KU-439-429

CONTENTS

Introduction

A new Age of Dragons is about to begin. The **powerful** creatures will return to rule the world once more, but this time it will be different. This time, they will have allies who will help them. Around the world, some young humans are making a strange discovery. They are learning that they were born with dragon blood – blood that gives them amazing powers.

CHAPTER 1
THE REFLECTION

"**T**aj!" shouted the boy's mother.

She **knocked** on his bedroom door. "Taj, hurry up. You'll be **LATE** for school."

"I'm coming! I'm coming," Taj called out to his mother.

The boy had not slept all **NIGHT**.

And he hadn't finished dressing for school.

He **stared** into a mirror on his wall.

He turned so that he could see the **reflection** of his back.

"Taj!" Shouted his mother. "What are you doing?"

The boy stared at the mirror without **MOVING**. He did NOT hear his mother.

Sadly, the boy took a deep **BREATH** and sighed. He kept staring at his back.

Growing from his shoulder
blades were two scaly WINGS.

CHAPTER 2
BELTS

That afternoon, after school, Taj **returned** to his room.

He made sure that his door was locked. Then he carefully pulled off his shirt.

He walked over to his **mirror**.

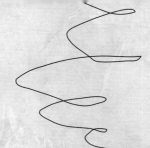

He had **wrapped** two sturdy belts around the pair of wings.

The belts held the wings tight to his body. The wings seemed to squirm and struggle under the belts.

The **BELTS** won't work forever, thought Taj.

What if they **fall** off when I'm at school?

What if the wings are only the **BEGINNING?** he thought.

What if the **SCALES** spread to the rest of my body?

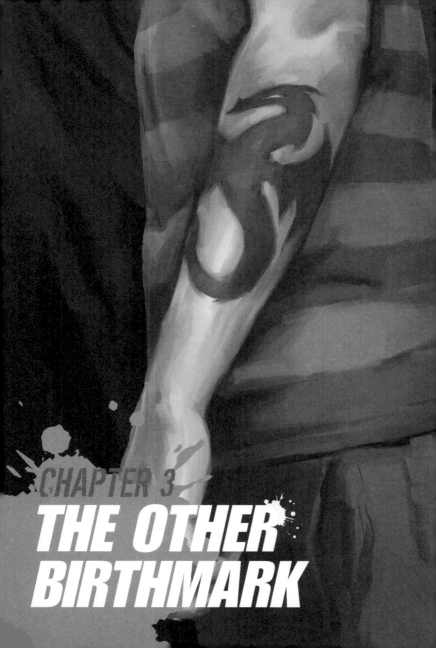

CHAPTER 3
THE OTHER BIRTHMARK

Taj scratched at the birthmark
on his arm. It was shaped like a
DRAGON.

He had seen that birthmark on
only one other person. His older
cousin **Kumar** had the mark, too.

Kumar **worked** at a fast food restaurant during the night.

Would Kumar know what to do?

The wings began to move again.

The belts **creaked** and groaned.

Taj pulled on a warm jumper
and *pushed* his back against the
wall. He could NOT wait any longer.

Taj listened at his door. Then
he put on a jacket and carefully
SLIPPED out of his window.

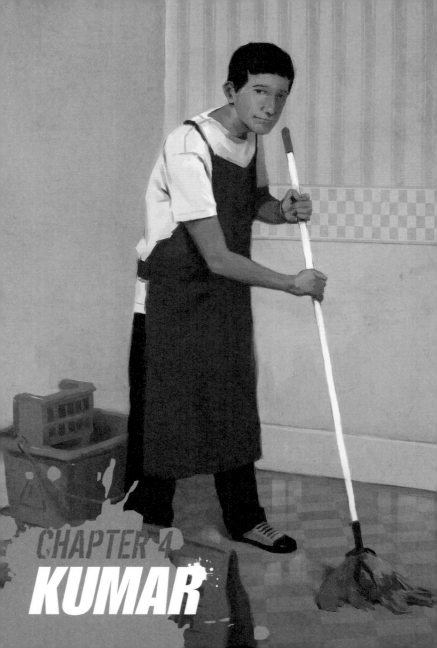

CHAPTER 4
KUMAR

Taj walked through the door of the NOISY restaurant.

He could see his COUSIN at the back of the room.

Kumar waved and smiled.

"Taj! he said. "Good to see you. What brings you here?"

Suddenly, Taj was **nervous**.

"I don't know," he said. He
scratched at his **BIRTHMARK** again.

Kumar noticed the **MARK** on his cousin's arm.

The older boy's face grew serious. "Don't say anything," he said to Taj. "I understand."

Kumar **shoved** a key into Taj's hand. "Here, go up to my room," said Kumar. "I'll be up as soon as I've finished cleaning. Go on. Don't worry."

Taj climbed the back **stairs**
to a flat high above the restaurant.

Kumar's rooms were small and
stuffy. **DARK** curtains were pulled
across the windows.

Taj's back began to **BURN** with
pain. The wings were moving
again, *pushing* against the belts.

CHAPTER 5
WINGS

He felt dizzy. The air in the room grew **HOT**.

Taj found a small bathroom. He rushed to the sink and splashed **WATER** on his face.

Then he turned, reaching for a towel. Taj's eyes grew **wide** with **TERROR**.

Hanging from the back of the door was a pair of wings. The scaly wings looked like his own, except that they were **WRINKLED** and dark.

"Taj, where are you?" called Kumar.

Taj's cousin was standing in the doorway to the flat. He held something **sharp** in his hand.

"I brought this from the restaurant," said Kumar. "Don't be AFRAID, cousin. I know how you feel. I felt the same way once. But I took care of it. Now I feel normal."

"No!" Taj yelled.

Crack! The belts holding his wings suddenly snapped apart.

The **WINGS** unfolded and seemed to fill the room.

Smash! Taj crashed through the window.

The wings *flapped* and carried him swiftly into the night.

Taj looked down at the bustling **CITY** below. He did not feel afraid. For the first time, he felt *calm* and peaceful.

He lifted his wings and headed towards home.

WINGED WONDERS

The cockatrice was a mythical beast from the Middle Ages. It looked like a large rooster with leathery wings and a lizard-like tail. Carrying a mirror was said to protect people from a **cockatrice**. The creepy rooster-serpent was so horrible that it would drop dead at the sight of its own reflection.

The **griffin** was another mythical monster of flight. The front half of the griffin was a monstrous eagle. The back half was a lion. The griffin would often swoop down to steal gold that people had dug out of mines. If no gold was available, it would take a human instead.

Another mythical bird was the **Phoenix**. The Phoenix myth first appeared in Egypt and the Middle East. The Phoenix was larger than an eagle, with a golden head and feathers of reds, purples, golds, and blues. When it grew old it would burst into flames and be reborn out of its own ashes.

Other cultures around the world have mythical birds as well. The Chinese believed in **Feng-huang**, a cross between a peacock and a pheasant. It was a sign of good luck if the Feng-huang appeared when a new king took the throne.

The Russian **Firebird** is another example of a mythical bird. It had eyes like crystals and wings like flames. A single feather would bring light to darkness.

ABOUT THE AUTHOR

Michael Dahl is the author of more than 200 books for children and young adults. He has won the AEP Distinguished Achievement Award three times for his non-fiction. His Finnegan Zwake mystery series was shortlisted twice by the Anthony and Agatha awards. He has also written the Library of Doom series. He is a featured speaker at conferences on graphic novels and high-interest books for boys.

ABOUT THE ILLUSTRATOR

After getting a graphic design degree and working as a designer for a couple of years, Federico Piatti realized he was spending far too much time drawing and painting, and too much money on art books and comics, so his path took a turn towards illustration. He currently works creating imagery for books and games, mostly in the fantasy and horror genres.

GLOSSARY

birthmark mark on the skin that has been there from birth

bustling busy, rushing around

reflection image shown on a shiny surface, like a mirror

scales small pieces of hard skin that cover the body of a reptile

scaly covered with small pieces of hard skin

serious thoughtful, not joking

sturdy strong and firm

DISCUSSION QUESTIONS

1. Why did Taj go to his cousin Kumar for help? Whom else could he have talked to?

2. Why do you think Taj was growing wings? What other physical transformations do you think he might have?

3. What happened to Kumar's WINGS? Why?

WRITING PROMPTS

1. Taj tries to **hide** his wings with belts. Write about a time you tried to hide something about yourself. What happened?

2. Taj respects and looks up to his older cousin. Choose a family member whom you respect. Why do you look up to that person? Write about them.

3. At the end of this book, Taj **flies** away. What do you think happens next? Write a chapter that describes what happens after this book ends.

MORE BOOKS TO READ

LIBRARY OF DOOM

Meet the mysterious Librarian. Keeper of the world's most dangerous books, sworn enemy of monsters made of paper and ink, crusader of young people threatened by ancient curses... Enter the Library of Doom to follow these heart-pounding adventures.